Underneath It All

SISTERHOOD CHRONICLES1

ANITA DAVIS

ISBN-10: 1-946721-00-X
ISBN-13: 978-1-946721-00-6

Books may be purchased in quantity by contacting the author Anita Davis:
Set Apart Publishing
PO Box 39229
Chicago, IL 60659
or by email at authoranitadavis@gmail.com

DEDICATION

There is so much that I can say to give honor to those who have helped me, but I will try to be as brief as possible. First, I give honor to the Trinity: the Father, the Son (Jesus), and the Holy Spirit for ordering my steps and getting me to this moment.

I want to express my sincerest gratitude to my mother, Evelyn Cole, for building my love of education, reading, and writing at an early age. My father, HLB III, for always being there for me.

Special, special thanks and gratitude go to my cousin Norman; my best friend Brandy; my best friend Tae Gilmore; my high school friend Joeysha Dobbins; my cousins Carlotta Baker, Dominique B., Rodney Williams, and Shana Simpson; my friend Victoria Brown; my sorority sister Asia Collins; my cousin and author, Tip Blockson. Thank you all. You each played an EXTREMELY significant role in helping me to complete and promote this novella. Thank you to anyone else who helped but I may not have mentioned by name.

"So many of our dreams at first seem impossible, then they seem improbable, and then, when we summon the will, they soon become inevitable."

*- **Christopher Reeve***

1

"Hello, sir. My name is Monica Sutton. My date, Jordan Smith, should be here already," Monica said excitedly to the maitre'd.

"Okay let me check…yes, I see that Mr. Smith has checked in already. Would you like for me to take your coat?"

"Yes, thank you."

"Your hostess, Rayna, will escort you to your seat now."

Monica inched closer and closer to her table and noticed that Jordan, with his chiseled jawline, smooth caramel skin, and onyx-hued eyes, was even more handsome than his pictures online. Rayna stopped four feet short of the table and alerted Jordan to Monica's arrival. They had chatted online for two days and talked on the phone for three weeks before they agreed to meet face to face. Now, his facial expression told it all; he was displeased with what he saw. Unsure of how the rest of the night would go,

Monica took her seat. She knew that the pictures she posted of herself on the website were from her neck up. She lied about her body type in the profile. She said that she was athletic. Every time he asked her for a full body picture, she would tell him that her camera was broken. He accepted this excuse every time, admitting that her voice was just too sexy and sultry for her to be lying about the way she looked.

"Hi, Jordan. How are you?" Monica said in that same sultry voice she had used whenever they talked on the phone. She extended her right hand to shake his.

"Hi, Monica. I'm uh, I'm okay." He was curt and shook her hand, averting eye contact.

"So how was your day?" Monica asked, hoping to engage him in conversation and make eye contact.

"It was very long. I'm exhausted." Jordan feigned a yawn.

"Oh, you sounded so energized when we spoke before I got here."

"Well, things have changed," Jordan said, not trying to mask the annoyance in his voice.

"Jordan, is everything okay?" Monica hoped that he wouldn't be shallow like all of the other men she fell for.

He paused. "Monica, you misled me. You had me thinking that you looked one way, but seeing you now, you're not who I imagined I've been talking to these past weeks. I'm not feeling this. I think it's best if I leave now. You can stay if you like. I'll leave enough to cover the bill."

Jordan excused himself from the table and headed straight for the door. Monica worked hard to hold back the tears that threatened to make her face their temporary home.

2

Pieces of Me

When I put the pen to the pad
It's supposed to relieve stress
But it's like the more I write, the more I get mad
Like I'm always being put to the test
Second guessing myself when I already know I'm
right
Trying hard to fight
The old me
Trying to birth a new we
Every time I think it's just starting
I find out it's ending
Then I'm back where I started in the beginning
Only now, I got a little bit more knowledge
To combat the folly that was once me when it came
to love.
Apparently I had it twisted
We would meet

Discover our compatibility
Then begin the bliss that would become we
But you proved me wrong
Cleverly pushing me away
While I was working hard to hold on
Racking my brain trying to come up with the best
way to make you stay
But you left me anyway

Writing poetry had become Monica's way of releasing her frustration—that and eating. She ate whatever she could get her hands on, which was a lot since she always managed to have her kitchen full of junk food and the delivery from local restaurants she had on speed dial. Her latest poem had been inspired by her recent failed attempt at love with Jordan. She knew that it was an unconventional way of meeting him, but she was willing to try it because she had exhausted all of her energy looking for love in the regular dating world, to no avail.

Any other Friday she would have rallied in front of her 55-inch LED TV and watch one romance movie after another, but tonight she had the pleasure of dining and dishing with her best friends at the Mellow Lounge. She grabbed a handful of Oreo cookies and headed down to the master bedroom. She passed her plush, king-sized bed and headed into her bathroom. Although she knew that she needed to look in the mirror to prepare herself, she hated having to because she never liked what she saw. Standing at five foot seven inches tall, Monica thought the 270 pounds that covered her body gathered inappropriately amid her waist, thighs, and arms. She never seemed to see what people saw when they called her pretty. She wondered if they attributed that adjective to her naturally wavy, shoulder-length hair; her slanted, hazel eyes; or her smooth, mocha colored skin. She just didn't see pretty when she looked in the mirror.

She slipped in and out of the shower in record time to prevent being late. After entering the closet in the bathroom, she surveyed her wardrobe to find an outfit for the night. Fortunately, it was fall in Chicago, and she wouldn't have to wear a heavy coat or snow boots, as the cold and snowy winters required. She especially appreciated not having to wear her puffy winter coat that seemed to make her look even bigger than what she already was. So, she opted for a pair of dark denim straight-leg jeans and her plum colored, loose-fitting sweater, which she hoped would mask her love handles. She thought that her gold earrings, a gold necklace, gold bangles, and camel-colored slouch boots would complete her ensemble. Once she was satisfied with her outfit and accessories, she went back to the mirror to do her make-up, pulling her hair back to have full access to her face. One thing she did appreciate about herself was that her skin was free of blemishes, so she never bothered to wear foundation, let alone buy it. She applied gold eye shadow to her lids, black mascara to her lashes, and put on her signature clear lip gloss. She thought that maybe her shiny lip gloss would deter a man's attention from her expansive waist, although that philosophy hadn't panned out when she met with Jordan.

***

Although there was a nip in the air, Monica didn't mind riding with the top down in her cherry red Sebring. The brush of the wind hitting her face and blowing through her hair always seemed to soothe her. At that point, it was helping to free her mind of some of the angst she had towards Jordan since seeing him the past Sunday, but that was quickly abated when she spotted a cute couple kissing on a park bench. Tension mounted again from rehashing what could have been between her and Jordan, making her speed to the Mellow Lounge and storm through the doors.

***

"Ooooo! I'm so mad at myself for liking him the way I did! Why can't I just meet a man that will like me for me and not for what I look like? Is that too much to ask?" Monica asked as she flopped down into her chair at the table.

"And hello to you, too!" Kim replied as she sipped some of her Long Island Iced Tea. Kim was the adventurous one.

"Sorry ladies, I'm just so tired of being manless. I thought that I would be married by now."

"Girl, you have to learn to be patient," Pam said. "You have so many other things going on in your life. Where do you have the time to squeeze in a man?" Pam Robinson was the studious and meticulous one of the bunch, only making calculated decisions. She couldn't trust her heart.

"I wouldn't have to make time for a man, he would be my life. I'll be thirty in a year, and I've never been in a relationship. You all already know my other major issue. Not only will I have to convince a man to look past my weight, but then once I get over that hump, I'm going to have to deny him of what every man eventually wants: a seed of his own.

"Stop being silly," Kim chimed in. "You're still young. You have all the time in the world to meet a man and fall in love. You can always adopt or get a surrogate mother. Hey, I'll even do that part for you. I won't have a husband to tell me what I can and can't do with my body because I'm never falling in love, let alone getting married. It's just not for me, and I'm perfectly fine with that."

"Kim, you say that now but I bet you'll be singing a different song years from now when you look back and see that you have no one to share all of your success with," Pam admonished.

"I bet I won't," Kim said, rolling her neck and sending her ebony hair cascading across her shoulders. She laughed and sipped more of her drink.

"Getting back to you, Ms. Monica, I told you about looking for a man. You should be waiting for God to send a man to you," Renee sputtered at Monica while sipping her Virgin Daiquiri. Renee Williams was the youngest of the four but had a spiritual maturity about her that made her the mother hen of the pack. She always managed to bring God into the conversation.

Kim and Renee were sisters, while Monica and Pam rounded out the quartet as friends. They all went to the same high school in Chicago, and even went to Howard University in Washington D.C. together. The test and trials they experienced together only proved to knit the bond of their sisterhood closer.

"Like I've said before, I trust God, but He said that faith without works is dead, so I'mma do my part in making sure I secure a man. A husband." Monica stared at them matter-of-factly.

The ladies all broke out in laughter after Monica's declaration. They continued to discuss other matters in each one of their lives.

Monica's thoughts drifted to one of her reoccurring fantasies of Kim and Renee's triplet brother, Keith. Of course, in the fantasy, she was a lot smaller. The latest fantasy played out at a formal gala. The sound of soft jazz filled the air as she sipped merlot. She would notice him staring greedily at her from across the room. In a floor-length, hip-hugging gown, she would glide across the room to him, where they would stare madly into each other's eyes before he whisked her away to a secluded balcony. There, he would kiss her feverishly before descending on one knee to propose to her. Right at the point he began to declare his need of having her in his life as his wife, Kim snapped Monica out of her daydream.

"Hello, earth to Monica." Kim laughed. "Didn't you hear me ask when you plan to perform some of your poetry? We've been dying to hear it."

"Now you know who she's thinking of when she gets that far-off look in her eyes." Pam said.

Kim, Renee, and Pam cooed in unison, "Keith."

"Oh shut up. I wasn't thinking about Keith. I was thinking about uh, uh…"

"Yes you were, we all know it, but we will leave that alone for now." Pam said.

"No, we won't." Kim decided to continue this particular conversation. "Monica, have you ever thought that if you would just be up front with Keith and tell him how you really feel, he might actually feel the same way you do?"

"Don't you think I've played the scenario over and over in my head, of confessing my love for him, him realizing that he felt the same way, and then us living happily ever after away from you nags?" Monica rolled her eyes and turned away from them to laugh.

"Well, you'll never know if you don't try," Kim snipped back.

"What I do know is that Keith would never want a hippo like me. I don't want to ruin the normalcy of our friendship by confessing how I feel and he not feel the same way. I'll just keep things the way they've always been between us, just friends."

"Monica, you have to stop putting yourself down like that. You are not a hippo. You're an intelligent, successful young woman who has so much to offer the world, if you would only recognize it," Renee said.

"Yes, I know that I am the best event planner, but in all the other areas of my life, I'm a loser." Monica's words faded as tears trickled down her face.

Pam scooted closer to Monica to comfort her while Kim reached out to wipe the tears from her face. Renee patted her dear friend's hand.

"Monica, you can't experience love with someone else until you first learn to love yourself. Since you think your insecurities seem to be tied to your weight, why don't you do something about it?" Renee said.

"Don't you think I've tried that several times? Guess what? I have failed each time. I ended up gaining weight instead of losing."

They often tried to convince her to go to the gym with them or change some of her eating habits but Monica's bouts of determination only lasted for so long before she was right back to her old bad habits with food and the lack of exercise.

"The last time you really gave it your all was in college, and the only reason you stopped working hard at your weight loss goal was because of Eric," Pam said.

Monica reflected back on her college days and the jerk, Eric, whom she had an extreme crush on. He was the first guy she had allowed herself to like since she realized her and Keith would never evolve into anything other than just being good friends. Eric and some of his friends always hung around the quartet. And, during that time, there was one particular incident with Eric that further scarred Monica's viewpoint of herself.

"Hey, Kim. Why do you always brush me off with your sexy self whenever I come around?" Eric cooed as he moved in closer to her.

"Maybe because I'm not interested in you." Kim stepped back to create more space between her and Eric.

"So you mean to tell me that you aren't attracted to me at all?" He inched in closer to her again.

"No, but my friend Monica is. I think you would really like her if you got to know her."

"Which one of your friends is Monica? Oh, wait I know which one, tubby over there." Eric pointed and laughed in Monica's direction.

"You insensitive jerk!" Kim stormed past Eric towards Monica.

Monica had heard their entire conversation, but her face and demeanor remained pleasant until she got back to her room that night and cried her eyes out over yet another man.

Pam continued to rub Monica's back bringing her back into the present time. "Monica, you have to stop letting your outer appearance dictate your self-worth. Happiness, real joy comes from within, but if you think that it's your weight that's hindering you from experiencing a better life, then, honey, you should do something about it. We're here to help you. We can't do it for you, but we're here to support you through it," Pam said, getting misty eyed.

Monica let the tears flow steadily as she contemplated whether or not she was strong enough to battle her demons with her eating habits. She knew the girls loved her and only wanted the best for her. They always encouraged her to love herself, no matter what size she was, and in that moment, she realized that it was time to start loving herself more.

Back in high school, Monica was the heaviest of the four, heavy being an understatement. Her frame nearly buckled under the excessive pounds that she dragged around. The more she was around them, with their slim figures, the more she buried her face in bags of chips, extra-large pizzas, all the treats Little Debbie had to offer, and heavy helpings of her mother's fattening meals. She dreaded going to college with them for fear of new surroundings and the possibility of their sisterhood dissolving, but they proved her wrong. They all seemed to be there for her no matter what.

"Okay, let's do it. Just promise to be patient but firm with me."

They all agreed to go workout with Monica the first thing the next morning. Since Kim worked out just about every day, she knew that there was a nutritionist on staff at her workout facility that would be able to assist Monica with a nutrition plan.

Although Monica didn't perform that night, the girls left satisfied, knowing that Monica was making steps toward a goal that would ultimately change her life and the way that she saw herself. They weren't concerned about Monica getting a man; they were more eager for her to see herself the way she was, beautiful inside and out.

3

The previous night had been a long and emotional one for Monica. All she wanted to do was sleep the morning away before she had to prepare for an event that evening.

Monica's phone rang.

"Monica, are you still asleep? Girl get up and get dressed. I'll be over to pick you up in thirty minutes," Kim squealed.

"I don't need you to pick me up. I can drive myself, and do you know what time it is?" Monica mumbled and stared at her alarm clock whose blue numbers read 6:15 a.m.

"I can't chance you driving yourself, you might not ever make it to the gym." Kim laughed. "And yes I know exactly what time it is, the beginning of a new you. Hurry up and get dressed and grab a banana or a piece of fruit, but nothing too heavy. I don't want you drudging along because you're too full."

"Kim, I don't even have fruit in my house. Oh wait, I do have some fruit cocktail in heavy syrup. Does that count?"

"No. Never mind. I'll just bring you something. Hurry, and we're definitely going to the grocery store after we leave the gym."

"Okay, I'm getting out of the bed and heading to my bathroom now. You happy?"

"Yup."

"Bye."

"Wait, before you hang up, do you even have workout gear?"

"Yes, Mommy Dearest. I may not use them, but I have them. Bye." Monica hung up the phone and rolled her eyes. She knew she needed to do this, she just wasn't sure if she was ready for the journey.

***

"Hey, girls." Kim eagerly greeted Pam and Renee as she and Monica walked up to them.

Pam and Renee had arrived just five minutes before Monica and Kim. They all greeted one another with hugs and kisses before entering the big glass doors that led them into the state of the art gym in downtown Chicago. Kim managed to get her personal trainer to come in and help establish a workout routine for Monica.

"Hi, Ron. These are my best friends Monica and Pam, and my sister, Renee."

"Hello, ladies. I'm Ron."

Except for Kim, the ladies couldn't help but gawk at Ron. He was beautifully sculpted from head to toe. His chocolate coated skin held on tightly to his very muscular six-foot frame. He had a low haircut, perfectly aligned white teeth, and mesmerizing almond shaped eyes. Ron checked the ladies in at the front desk, and then escorted them to the cardio section of the gym. They all gave their full attention to his bowlegged walk as they followed behind him. He took them through a stretch routine to relax their muscles before he demanded that they each complete thirty minutes on the treadmill. The time on the treadmill was like a quick walk in the park for Renee and Pam. Kim even ran the entire time on the treadmill, but Monica struggled to endure.

Panting, Monica said, "Okay, I think I've had enough." She braced her feet on the outer parts of the treadmill and draped her upper body across the display board.

"Monica, I know this may be difficult since it's your first time, but if you keep at it, it should get easier," Pam said in between short breaths as she ran on the treadmill next to Monica's.

The ladies continued to encourage Monica. Ron realized that being on the treadmill seemed daunting for Monica, so he encouraged her to focus on the end result, what she would ultimately gain. She reminded herself of her fantasies of Keith and gave it all she had until her time ended.

Monica thought that the workout was over as she stepped down from the treadmill with sweat covering every inch of her body, but Ron assured her that her time on the treadmill was only the beginning. He then escorted the ladies over to the strength training machines and gave them a few exercises to complete so that he could give his undivided attention to Monica.

Ron took Monica through a standard full body routine of strength training to begin to tone her muscles from her shoulders to her ankles. When he felt that she had truly exhausted herself, he motioned for her to stop doing crunches and helped her up to her feet.

"So, Monica, what areas of your body do you feel you need to work on the most?"

"Do I even have to tell you the answer to that question? You have eyes, don't you?" Monica dropped her head.

"It's important for me to know what you think. Each person has a certain way they envision themselves. I may tell you what you need to work on, but then you might have a completely different opinion. I don't want to bombard you with my opinion alone. I want us to come to an agreement as to what you want to work on and how you want to look." Ron stared intently at Monica.

"Thank you. I appreciate that. Well, overall I want to lose weight to be slimmer. More attractive." Monica looked down.

"You do know that you are beautiful, don't you?'

"I bet you say that to a lot of women." Monica's dark complexion masked her red cheeks.

"Only to the ones I think are truly beautiful." Ron smiled. "Any other changes you want to make?"

"I want my arms to not be flabby anymore. I want to wear a belt and it not disappear when I sit. I want my thighs to not be so friendly and rub on each other so much. I want to sit and be able to cross my legs at my thighs and not just my ankles. There are so many changes that I want to make about my body," Monica uttered with her head still down.

Ron touched Monica's chin to lift her head. "And that's all perfectly fine as long as you understand that it is going to take a lot of hard work and will power to get to where you want to be. I don't want you to think of this as a diet but rather a lifestyle change."

Monica was comforted by the kindness in Ron's eyes and the way he spoke to her.

"Kim told me that you plan to see the nutritionist today as well. It is extremely important that you be honest with the nutritionist about your eating habits so that she can create a meal plan that will work for you and not against you. Would you be interested in continuing personal training with me? I would love to help you."

"Yes. I would appreciate that. Thank you so much." Monica smiled at the promise of losing weight and being around Ron more.

"Okay, so by the time you're done with the nutritionist I'll have the different fitness training packages printed out for you. You can pick the best option that fits your budget, and we can set a schedule for your one on one workouts with me. See you in a bit."

The other ladies were engrossed in their workout as Monica signaled that she was headed to see the nutritionist.

***

Monica met Kim at the front door of the workout facility about thirty minutes later.

"So how did it go with the nutritionist?" Kim asked as she pulled out of the gym's parking lot.

"It went great. I love the staff here. She gave me a meal plan that I should be able to stick to if I actually plan to lose the weight. We'll just see how things go."

"Monica what do you mean, 'if' you actually plan to lose the weight? You're committed to this, right?" Kim paused, choosing her words carefully before speaking again, "we love you just the way you are, but we know that you want to change the way you look. That can only happen if you put in the work. It won't be easy, but it'll be worth it," Kim admonished as she pulled up in front of Monica's house.

"I know it'll be worth it, but I'm just not sure that I can do it," Monica said exasperatedly.

"Yes, you can Monica, and you will. We're here to support you."

"I know you all are, but this is something I suspect I will have to do on my own." Stiff, sore, and exhausted, Monica struggled to get out of the car, but Kim stopped her.

"Wait, I brought you home but I forgot that we need to go to the grocery store. Get back in."

"No Kim, that's okay. I can take myself." Monica knew that Kim meant well but she really just wanted to go in the house and soak her aching body.

"Monica, I know you can, but we already agreed this morning that we would go together. I'm traveling this road with you whether you like it or not." Kim hated how Monica could be so stubborn at times.

"Kim, I said that I can take myself. I won't even go in the house first. I'll just get in my car with my list and go to the store and get the things I need."

In a sing-song voice, Kim said, "Monica, must you forget how long we've been friends? Either I take you, or I follow you there to make sure you go. One way or the other you're going to the grocery store now to get the food you need."

Monica reluctantly closed the car door, knowing that Kim would make good on her promise. They made it to the store, grabbed enough food to sustain Monica for the next two weeks, and left. Kim helped Monica carry the bags in the house before they hugged each other goodbye.

4

Between years of attempting to diet, and the nutritionist and Ron's advice, Monica knew what she needed to do to be successful this time around. She started putting away the fresh produce, vegetables, and lean meat she got from the store. She threw away every fattening item of food in her house. Then, she started to smell herself from the hard workout, so she rushed upstairs to shower. After showering, she decided to prepare some meals for the next couple of days to ensure that there would always be something available to eat when she was hungry, rather than being tempted to go to a fast food restaurant. It was difficult for her to cook initially because she was so used to fattening ingredients like lard, but she opted to use olive oil whenever a recipe called for some type of grease or oil.

After she prepared her food, she retreated to her den to relax. Monica was compelled to write a poem about her issues with food and her weight.

This Affair

This ongoing affair I have with food consumes me.
It has devoured my attention and heightened my emotional sensitivity.

I can't adorn myself with certain clothes at most times,
Because my body can get comparable to that of an elephant's behind.

One moment I'm on a healthy-eating-lifestyle high,
But the next I'm at the Cheesecake Factory indulging in the entire pie.

Because of this world-wind affair, my body expands and contracts as it may,
Depending on if I allow my eating habits and lack of exercise to get in disarray.

It's not enough to turn a blind eye to fast food places as I go to and fro,
I have to be so selective about what foods I allow to enter my abode.

*You would think after several interventions with
the gym and fasts,*
*I would have ended this affair with my love
secluded to the past.*

*I should know by now this tryst will be never
ending,*
*I just have to learn to deal with it to keep my
shape from over-extending.*

***

Monica had never realized that exercising could be so addictive. It was now Tuesday, and she had managed to work out seven times. Although Ron challenged her strength and endurance in her morning training sessions, she had been opting to go back to the gym for more cardio in the evenings. It was 8 p.m. and she had just returned from working out when her phone rang.

"Hello. How are you doing, Monica?"

"Oh, hey, Kim, I'm doing fine. How are you?"

"Kim is not the only one on the line," Pam said and Renee mumbled a similar sentiment.

"Sorry, ladies. How are you all doing?"

"We're fine," Kim, Renee, and Pam said collectively.

"We just wanted to check up on you to see how everything is going with sticking to your 'getting fit' plan."

"Everything's okay."

"What's wrong, honey? You don't sound too convincing," Renee said.

"Well, I know it's only been four days since I really started working out. I know if I keep this up then I should see improvements, but I don't yet and that's kind of wearing on me. I've been working out two times a day and I don't see any changes and…" Monica let her words trail off, hesitating to say what else was bothering her.

"Like you said, it's only been four days, but as long as you're committed to sticking to it this time, you'll start to see the results soon enough," Pam chimed in.

"Is there something else bothering you?" Kim questioned Monica's previous hesitation to speak.

"I know you all probably get tired of me talking bad about myself, but it's just become so natural to me. I'm in the gym and I get in my zone working out hard, but then when I look up and see all those beautiful women with their slim Coca-Cola bottle shapes and all the attention they get from the men in there, I just want to run out. Why can't I be like them?"

ANITA DAVIS

"Monica, you can't worry about how those women look or how they're being looked at. You have to focus on you. The Bible says in Matthew 6:33, 'But seek ye first the kingdom of God, and his righteousness; and all these things shall be added unto you.' You have to stop worrying about how you look. Just focus on maturing your relationship with God. He'll give you the strength and courage to continue your weight loss journey, and He'll bless you with a man when the time is right," Renee said, hoping to encourage Monica to focus more on God and less on her weight or a man.

Monica rolled her eyes in response to Renee's advice before she responded, "Thanks, Renee but-" Monica had another incoming call. It was Ron. "Sorry ladies, I have to take this call on the other line. Talk to you all soon."

Monica ended the phone conversation with the ladies and answered her other line. *Is he calling to cancel our session in the morning?*

"Hello, may I speak to Monica?" His deep bass voice flowed through the phone.

"Hi." Monica giggled. "You never have to ask for me when you call, I'm the only one who will answer."

"I didn't want to assume, but that's good to know. Sorry to call you so late, but I was just calling to check on you and see how everything's going with the workouts being so strenuous. How are you holding up with your new eating plan?" Ron said, feigning deep concern for Monica's well-being.

"Oh, I'm doing great. Thanks for asking. I'm learning so much from you in our sessions and you know I've been going back for a second helping of working out in the evenings when my schedule permits."

"Speaking of schedules, that's what I was calling you about. Your schedule. Do you think that you can pencil me in for dinner tomorrow night?"

Baffled, Monica didn't know how to respond. She wasn't sure if she had heard him correctly. "Hunh?"

"I hope I'm not being too forward. I usually don't ask any of my clients out, but you're just so irresistible. Will you have dinner with me tomorrow night?"

Monica almost fell off the couch in shock as she gathered her wits to respond. *Me, irresistible?* No man had ever said that to her before. She glowed.

Ron waited with a smirk on his face hoping that Monica was buying what he was selling her; a night with him that he hoped would end in mind-blowing sex. He always thought that the ones with low self-esteem were the best women to have. They never complained about how he treated them and what he asked of them. They were just so content that he chose them.

Monica decided to reply before he recanted his offer, "Yes, I would be more than happy to have dinner with you tomorrow." Monica had concluded that maybe her workouts and change of eating habits were showing off after all. She surmised that as the only reason Ron would want to be seen outside of the gym with her.

'Okay, so I'll pick you up around seven tomorrow night. Goodnight."

"Goodnight." Monica beamed.

Monica wanted to call the girls back, especially Renee, and tell them that she had a date and possibly, a man. However, she decided not to, fearing that she might jinx what could become of her and Ron.

***

Ron picked up Monica as promised the next night. He took her to Olive Garden and laid the compliments on thick all night long.

"I had a great time tonight." Ron smiled as he walked Monica to her front door.

"So did I," Monica said, beaming with excitement.

"I guess this is goodnight, hunh?"

"It doesn't have to be," Monica said, shyly looking down.

Ron understood what Monica was implying and began kissing her on her neck as Monica fumbled to put the key in the door. Once the door was open and Monica had disarmed the alarm, Ron groped and kissed her deeply.

Monica didn't want the attention she was getting from Ron to end, so she escorted him to her bedroom.

He couldn't see his way around so he tried turning on the light, but Monica quickly led him to the bed without the lights being turned on. She didn't want him to see her body. Ron had become fully undressed and was working diligently for Monica to do the same, but after moments of tussling with her just to remove her pants, he figured it was slowing down the process, so he laid her down. He put on a condom, quickly entered her and thrusted in and out of her until he reached his climax.

5

Between Monica's workout sessions in and out of the gym with Ron and the events she planned, she had become extremely busy, which had left no time to hang out with her girls. The rest of the sisterhood was trying to put an end to Monica's disappearance.

"Why is it the only way we can talk to you now-a-days is by phone? We miss you, Monica," Kim spoke up first.

The ladies had continued their weekly girls' night at the Mellow Lounge on Friday nights and had now added Sunday brunch to their bonding time. But, it had been a while since they'd last seen Monica.

"Sorry, ladies. I've just been so busy with work and my new boyfriend." Monica squealed.

"Excuse me, your new boyfriend? It's only been two months since we've seen you and about two weeks since we all talked together on the phone.

How can you have claimed a boyfriend in such short time?" Renee asked, baffled by Monica's admission.

"Oh, Monica, I'm so happy for you," Pam exclaimed.

"And what do you have to say, Kim?" Monica asked, worried that all her friends might not support her newfound happiness.

"Well, you know me, I can't and won't give my heart to anyone. I want you to be happy, and if you feel like this guy is making you happy enough to call him your man, then I'm happy for you." Kim spoke with little enthusiasm knowing that until Monica loved herself she would never attract a man that would fully love her the way she deserved to be loved.

"Thank you all so much, except for Renee. You questioning my relationship is not needed. You always manage to try and kill my joy. I won't let you this time around. Ron and I are so happy together."

"Wait, did you say Ron? Ron your trainer? How did that happen?" Pam asked with her eyes bulging from their sockets.

"Well, remember that Tuesday we were on the phone right after I started working out?" They each nodded their heads. "Well, he was the caller that interrupted our conversation. He asked me out to dinner the following night and we've been seeing each other ever since."

"So is he as serious about you as you are him? Does he claim that you two are in a committed relationship?" Renee inquired.

"No, but it won't be long before he does." Monica rolled her eyes in annoyance.

"Monica, if he doesn't feel the way you do, then maybe you need to slow down your emotions just to make sure you don't get hurt," Pam cautioned.

"It's too late for that. I already love him."

"What?" Renee asked shockingly.

"Yes, you heard me right, I love him. He's been the only constant man in my life. We communicate every day."

"Does that include your training sessions?" Renee asked, smoothing out her eyebrows in frustration.

"Yes, but—"

Monica was interrupted by Renee's further interrogation, "but, nothing. What do you all do when he's not training you? Where does he take you? Have you met his family?"

Tired of Renee's nagging, Monica said, "look ladies, I still have some more details to finalize for my event for Saturday. I would love for you all to come to it. I'll text all the details. Talk to you later."

Monica hung up the phone, but the others remained on their lines.

"You know she's not telling us everything, right?" Renee stated matter-of-factly.

"Stop being so hard on her, Renee. I believe that as she continues her weight loss journey, her inner image will eventually change. You know, the way she sees herself." Kim said confidently about Monica finding her way.

"I want to believe that too, but I just don't want her to make mistakes that she can't undo later," Renee said.

"I agree with both of you, but ultimately it's up to Monica to decide who she will and won't date and how she sees herself. As her friends, we just have to make sure that we're there to support her through it all."

"You're right too, Pam. Goodnight ladies," Kim said.

They all hung up their phones after saying a quick prayer that Monica wouldn't get more emotional scars as a result of dealing with Ron.

***

For as much as the girls knew about Monica, they didn't know how sexually active she had been in recent years. It's not that she slept with every man she came in contact with, but rather, she had sex with the men she pursued relationships with, hoping that would keep them around. Time after time, she learned that that wasn't the answer, yet she couldn't seem to pull herself out of the habit of being that way. Over the course of the past three years, she could count on one hand the amount of men she had been with, but according to her mother and Renee's standards, that was way too many. Monica grew up in a Baptist home, attending church on Sundays and bible class on Wednesday nights. Her mother made her read the Bible every day. So she knew what it said about the whole concept of sex before marriage, but she figured God would forgive her in due time. She believed her method of allowing a man to sample the milk before he bought the cow would be beneficial for her. She tried to use sex to get and keep a man. Although the theory hadn't worked out for her yet, she was willing to keep trying until it did. Monica knew deep down in her heart that her ideology wasn't the best way, but she felt at this point in her life and with the way she looked, it was currently her only method for getting the results she wanted—a man.

6

Renee, Pam, and Kim received Monica's text, giving them explicit details of where the event was and how to dress for the breast cancer dinner that Monica's company had been hired to coordinate.

The ladies all looked gorgeous in their own right. Renee wore a floor-length black dress with a sequined shawl. Pam donned a charcoal trumpet style dress that further narrowed her already tiny waist. Kim of course, as daring as she was, opted to wear an electric blue fitted floor length mermaid style gown that seemed to hug every curve on her body. She loved all of the attention she was getting from men around the room. It was cocktail hour so they stood around with their champagne flutes, while of course Renee sipped on sparkling juice. They made small talk and enjoyed each other's company as they turned down numerous offers from male suitors while waiting to spot Monica.

"I can't believe it's been two whole months since we've seen her. We've never gone this long without seeing one another," Kim said.

"I know right, but we couldn't help the fact that she's been as busy as she's been, especially if she had to coordinate this beautiful event," Pam said as she looked around in awe of the elegant ballroom painted ivory and antique gold with big, breathtaking chandeliers hanging all around.

"Well, it wasn't just this event or her new exercise regimen that has kept her from us. I believe that it has more to do with Ron. There's just something not right about him. I can sense it in my spirit. If she keeps this up with him, things won't turn out for the best for her where he's concerned. I just know it," Renee said, worried about her dear friend.

"While we thank you for always having your ear to the Lord, Renee, we can't make Monica do anything. Like Pam said, we can only be there to support her as things happen in her life. Since it's such a beautiful night, please don't put a downer on it by preaching to Monica when we see her." Kim laughed to ease the tense air around them.

Renee rolled her eyes at Kim and laughed as she sipped more of her sparkling juice.

"That woman is wearing that dress," Pam said as she stared at a woman about twenty feet in front of her.

"What woman are you referring to?" Kim spun around trying to see who might be competition for her that night. While she didn't plan to give her number to a man, she did enjoy all the attention she was getting and wasn't ready to share it with any other woman.

"The one in that deep purple, fitted ruched dress directly in front of us. Her back is facing us."

"Oh, that woman." Kim did have to admit that the woman's full-figured Coca-Cola shape accentuated by the fit of the dress might prove to be some strong unspoken competition for her that night.

Kim was almost tempted to go introduce herself to her new rival when the woman turned around and proved to be Monica. Kim, Renee, and Pam gasped as they saw how stunning Monica looked. It's not that they didn't always think that she was pretty, but at that moment, she had a certain confidence about herself that they were unfamiliar with.

Monica noticed them all standing there with their eyes big and mouths open wide with shock as she glided over to embrace them. She hugged each one of them, giving them air kisses to ensure that they wouldn't mess up each other's makeup. She hugged Kim last.

Kim let Monica go, stepped back, stared at her, and then hugged her again. "Oh my God, Monica! You look amazing. How much weight have you lost so far?"

"You think I've lost weight?" Monica asked, not exuding the same confidence she had just executed when talking with constituents of the city council.

"We think? We know," Pam chimed in with her hand on her hip. "Why question the fact that you look amazing?"

"I've missed seeing you all so much and to answer your question Kim, I've lost about twenty-five pounds, but this girdle I have on is doing an amazing job." The ladies all laughed. "You all have never seen me in the capacity of an event planner. I don't know why, but for the life of me I manage to have all of this confidence when I walk around the room greeting the guests, but then I go home and cry because I'm so lonely."

"Lonely? I thought you had a 'boyfriend'?" Renee said.

Kim gave Renee a cold stare that informed her not to share her wary feelings of Ron. Renee understood and changed her demeanor.

Monica spoke to hush Renee. "I meant before Ron, I felt lonely." They all knew that she was lying; she still felt that way, and they could each see it in her eyes.

"So how are things going with Ron? You rushed off the phone with us the other night," Pam asked, hoping that Monica would give more insight into what she had going on with Ron.

"Everything's great, just great." Monica managed to muster up a smile as she replied.

"So then, why is Ron gawking at and practically falling over that woman over there?" Renee asked annoyed.

"Oh, that's nothing. Ron is a bit of a flirt. That's how he continues to build his clientele."

"Monica, he has his hand on the small of her back almost touching her butt. It's not that loud in here. Why does he need to keep leaning in and whispering to her? I'm telling you, Monica, I don't like him for you."

"Well, gratefully I didn't ask you, Renee," Monica said, fuming. "Sometimes you just need to mind your own business."

"I only want what's best for you, and he's not it!" Renee replied hastily at Monica.

"Renee, let me help to clear your vision since it's gotten a little fuzzy over the years. You've made some of the same mistakes I've made when it comes to men. As I recall, you got your abortion a week ahead of mine, and you were right back with that fool the next day. He continued to beat on you and yet you stayed with him, for what, another year? It's obvious by the way you go around condemning me that you have forgotten your own sin. So before you keep looking into my eyes trying to tell me what to do, please take the speck out of yours."

Renee was speechless. Her secret between her and Monica was out.

Monica returned her attention to Pam and Kim. "I am so glad that you two could come tonight, please enjoy yourselves. You have to excuse me now though, I need to go check on some things." Monica pivoted on her heels and stormed off.

Pam and Kim both turned towards Renee, who was now beet red, although her dark complexion masked it. Shock covered Pam and Kim's face while shame covered Renee's, but before either Pam or Kim could utter words, Renee decided to speak up. Choking on her words and doing a poor job of holding back her tears, she muttered, "I can't deal with this right now. I have to go." Renee raced off towards the coat room. Pam and Kim decided not to chase after her. They were too stunned and confused to do so. Guests were being ushered to their seats for the event to begin. Pam and Kim followed suit, but not before noticing Ron and the woman he was all over earlier making their exit to a nearby stairway.

***

Monica was happy with the way the event panned out. It was a beautiful evening, and she had managed to raise one million dollars towards the fight for a cure for breast cancer, however, happiness wasn't what she felt for telling Renee's secret. She hadn't wanted to share it, she loved Renee and had promised to keep it between the two of them, but she was so tired of Renee always getting on her as if she didn't have demons and issues of her own to deal with. They'd been friends for too long and had endured too much together to end it. She would have to find a way to repair the breach she might have caused in their friendship.

Her "relationship" with Ron kept her on edge. She shouldn't have been so sprung on him since they had actually only gone to dinner that one time. Every other time they met was either at the gym or in bed. For the first two weeks he seemed to come over every day for some of her helpings, but in weeks past it had dwindled down to once a week and that was only because she practically begged him to come over. She would have to offer him sexual favors that no other woman seemed to do the way she did. He would come over and she would let him sex her the way he wanted to and would then treat him to amazing oral sex, hoping he would spend the night and hold her, but he never did. He would leave soon after she was done pleasing him. She knew he wasn't the best for her, but he was the only man paying any kind of attention to her so she wanted to hold on to him as long as possible.

It was one o'clock in the morning and Monica decided to call Ron, hoping that he would come over. After six times of trying to call him with no answer, she rested on the fact that she would just have to wait to see him in the next morning at their training session.

***

Monica entered the gym that morning excited to weigh in, work out, and see the piece of a man she had. She swiped her card and was prepared to walk away from the counter when the head manager stopped her.

"Ms. Sutton, may I have a moment with you?"

Monica nodded and the manager escorted her over to a corner.

"Ms. Sutton."

"You can call me Monica." She paused to read the woman's nametag before speaking, "Sherry."

"How has everything been going for you since you've joined our facility?"

"It's been great. I love it here. The staff is so nice and I just love my trainer Ron. I don't want to be late for my session this morning, so I need to get over there to him." Monica scanned the gym searching for Ron. He wasn't in their usual spot.

"I'm glad to hear that you're satisfied with our customer service. Speaking of Ron, he called in to give me his resignation this morning, so I am turning over his clients to other trainers. If it's all right with you, you will now be with April. She's very good and should help you to continue to reach your goal. She'll be with you in a moment. Please let me know if there is anything else I can do for you." Sherry walked away wondering why Monica looked like she had just been told that someone had died. For Monica, something did die; more of her self-esteem.

7

Monica didn't work out after she was told Ron resigned. She stopped by a fast food restaurant and ordered a big breakfast before heading home. She tried calling Ron, but the voice on the other end said the number was no longer in service. She was devastated, wondering why he resigned and now his phone was disconnected. She had no way to get in contact with him. It dawned on her that she didn't even know where he lived. She scarfed all of her food down and then buried herself under her covers as she cried herself to sleep.

Hours later, Monica was awakened by her phone. Disoriented, she fumbled to answer it. She didn't even bother to look at the caller ID.

"Ron, is this you, baby?"

"Girl, naw this ain't Ron. And I ain't your baby," Kim said, laughing.

Monica remained solemn. "Kim, what do you want?"

"Reminding your slimming tail to make sure that you meet us for brunch today."

"Oh, I forgot about that. Look, I can't make it today," Monica said, not wanting to be bothered with anyone other than Ron.

"Monica, we're not taking no from you as an answer anymore. You have been dodging spending time with us for the past two months. You're coming with us today and you *are* going to enjoy yourself," Kim commanded.

Monica knew that Kim's tone meant business and that she would very well drag her out of the bed, if necessary. She gave in, knowing that she wouldn't win. "What time and where again?" Monica rolled her eyes and huffed.

"Since you sound so out of it, we'll push back the time until two o'clock, and meet us at that Italian restaurant on the west end of Yorktown Mall."

Monica hung up the phone and buried herself back under the covers.

***

Hours later, Monica dragged herself out of bed, dressed, and headed over to the restaurant. She was the second to last one to be seated at the table with the ladies. She greeted Pam and Kim, each with a hug and kiss on the cheek.

Pam and Kim had tried calling Renee all morning long but she never answered the phone. The two were both shocked when Renee finally entered the restaurant and made her way to their table. Renee greeted Pam and Kim each with a hug and kiss on the cheek. She took a seat opposite of Monica and sat with her arms folded, boring holes into her. She wasn't upset with her, but she was hurt. Monica had exposed her secret. Renee knew she should have long since told Pam and Kim, but she could never muster up the courage to do so; she didn't know how they would react. She only told Monica after she'd had one of her own, because she felt Monica understood the emptiness of losing a child.

Pam and Kim allowed their friends to stare at one another for minutes before they decided to break the silence.

"It's been so long since we've had the chance to just sit and talk and enjoy each other's company. Wouldn't you agree, Kim?" Pam asked, sounding rehearsed.

"Yes, I love the fact that we're all here, together, as friends who have gone through so much. What we go through should only make our bond stronger, not tear us apart," Kim said, hoping to get through to Monica and Renee.

Renee finally decided to speak, but continued to stare at Monica, her stare softened. "You're right,

Kim. We have been through too much. I spent all night praying and crying out to God asking Him to forgive me of the horrible thing I did when I killed my unborn child to appease that jerk, Ted. I've been trying to be right with God ever since I committed that awful act. He showed me last night that while He had forgiven me when I first asked Him, I had yet to forgive myself. That's why I'm not mad at you. I had been condemning myself for so long, that it seemed as if I started condemning you as well." Renee reached out to grab Monica's hand. "I'm so sorry for seeming like I'm always on you, but I know what we've been through with the whole abortion deal. I don't want us to ever suffer anything close to the pain that we've already endured. While we each had different reasons for doing what we did, the pain of it is still real to us. I knew that you were making so much progress with your weight loss and I didn't want Ron to mess it up. I'm sorry if I've hurt you. Can you forgive me?" Renee cried as she continued to hold Monica's hand.

The waiter had approached the table and noticed the exchange between the ladies. He signaled to Kim that he would return.

Monica paused before speaking. "Renee, I forgive you. I'm not mad at you. I had just gotten so tired of you always berating me that I just snapped. I'm so sorry for blabbing your secret. Can you please forgive me?" Monica cried and squeezed Renee's hands.

"Yeah. So are we good now?" Renee asked Monica.

"Yes, forever and a day." Renee and Monica stood up and embraced each other as their tears continued to flow. They soon returned to their seats.

"I hate to break up you all's love fest, but Renee, why didn't you tell me about the abortion? I'm your sister, your triplet, I would've been there for you," Kim said, hurt.

Renee noticed Kim's demeanor. "I'm so sorry, Kim, for not trusting you with what I was going through at that time, but I never planned to tell a soul about what I had done. You were already on me about breaking up with Ted because of his abuse towards me. I didn't want you to think any lower of me than you already did. After Monica had confided in us about her abortion, I felt that she was the only one that I could talk to about it. I knew she would understand and not judge me. She knew my pain. I'm glad that it's finally out though. I feel free, like a weight has been lifted off of me."

"It's okay, Renee. Just like we didn't judge Monica, we wouldn't have judged you either. We love you forever and a day, too." All four ladies stood and hugged each other. They shed tears of joy before taking their seats. The waiter returned to take their orders. Pam, Kim, and Renee each ordered pasta entrees and side salads. Monica was a different story.

"I'll have the shrimp scampi fritta, lasagna fritta's. Oh, and can I have extra Alfredo sauce with that? Also, can I have the stuffed mushrooms and the grilled sausage and peppers rustica? And I'll have a Skinny Martini, not that I'm skinny or trying to be." Monica laughed.

The waiter left the table while Kim, Pam, and Renee stared incredulously at Monica.

"What?" Monica asked them, hunching her shoulders.

"Monica, are you okay, honey? You just ordered enough food to feed a small village in Africa. Is everything okay?" Pam asked, worried.

"Yes, everything is perfectly fine." Monica snapped and signaled for the waiter.

"Yes, Aaron, can I please have my drink now?"

"Yes, ma'am. I'll bring it right back to you."

Monica began to tap her fingernails against the table while the other three stared at her.

Renee decided to speak next. "Monica, are you sure that everything is okay between us? You still seem very much on edge."

"You and I are fine, Renee. I know how much food I ordered, Pam, and I plan to eat it all right here at this table." Monica continued to tap her fingernails on the table.

"Honey, you've been doing so well with working out and eating right. Why would you want to ruin all your hard work by going back to drowning whatever emotional issues you're having in food?" Kim inquired.

"I just don't get it." Monica huffed, with her elbows resting on the table. She let her head fall into her hands and then sat up to face them all again. "I've lost twenty-five pounds thus far. I know that I am not as slim as you all are, but I thought that I would be getting more attention from men by now. The men at the gym all smile at me, but I can tell that their looks are more out of pity or 'way to go' than for an attraction to me. Then there was Ron."

Pam and Kim looked at each other with raised eyebrows.

"What about Ron?" Kim asked, hoping that Monica already knew about him hooking up with the woman the night before. Neither Kim nor Pam wanted to be the ones to break the news to Monica.

"Ron, what about Ron? I knew he wasn't the one for me but he showed an interest in me and I just ran with it. You were right, Renee."

Renee patted Monica's hand in solace. "I didn't want to be right about him, honey, but I just knew in my spirit that he wasn't for you."

"It just hurts to know that even when I'm intimate with a man, he still doesn't want to be with me. He didn't answer my calls last night. I went to the gym this morning only to find out that he had resigned. I went home and tried to call him again and discovered that his phone had been disconnected. He didn't even give me the courtesy of telling me that we were over. After all I've done for him, he couldn't even tell me we were through to my face. What is wrong with me? Why continue to lose weight if my weight isn't the issue? Maybe this is God punishing me for the abortion. Maybe I'm destined to be alone for the rest of my life." Monica grabbed a napkin, bowed her head, and began to wipe away the tears that flooded her face.

Pam rubbed Monica's back.

Renee spoke up. "You've been looking at this the wrong way, honey. You're not losing weight to get a man. You're supposed to be losing weight to build a better you. You can't just go to the gym and workout and eat right. You have to feed your spirit with the Word of God as well. When was the last time you studied the Bible? When was the last time you talked to God? Monica, you know who God is. You have to ask Him to show you the way to live your life. Ask Him for patience. Monica, you have to work on the inside of you just as much as you've been doing the outside of you."

Monica couldn't stop crying thinking about how long it had actually been since she had talked to God. She grew up knowing Him but she seemed to part ways with Him after having the abortion. She knew what Renee said was right.

Renee suggested the ladies all join hands and bow their heads. She led them in a prayer, thanking God for what He had done in each of their lives, asking Him to forgive them of their sins, and to guide them as they moved forward in life. Monica felt the most relieved after they said, *Amen*, in unison.

The waiter returned with their food. Monica asked if the waiter could forgive her for ordering so much food but that she only wanted the shrimp scampi she had ordered. The waiter obliged her and took back the remaining food she didn't want.

The ladies all began to savor their food, but as usual Kim just couldn't be quiet. She always had to be the one to talk about any and everything. "Guess what, Pam and Monica?"

Pam and Monica looked at each other worried, not knowing what Kim might reveal. Pam and Monica then looked at Renee, hoping she would give them a clue, but all Renee did was smile and continued chewing.

"Keith is moving back here to Chicago," Kim said.

Pam squeaked. "Yay. I know that your family is so excited after him being gone away for so long, working in California. What made him change his mind about deciding to move back?"

Kim paused, trying to read Monica's stoic face before she continued talking. "Well, he finally admitted that he missed being around his family. He's ready to start a family of his own and he wants his family to be rooted and reared in Chicago like he was."

"Did you hear Kim, Monica? Keith is moving back to Chicago. Aren't you happy to hear that?" Renee asked, wondering why Monica was so quiet and tense at the mention of Keith moving back to Chicago.

"No."

"Why not?" Pam asked.

"You ever heard of the saying 'Out of sight, out of mind'?" Monica asked.

"Yes," Pam, Kim, and Renee said in unison as usual.

"That's how I've handled my feelings for Keith. Since he's been out of my sight, I try to keep him out of my mind. Granted, that doesn't work most of the time, but I still try it, nonetheless. It's been one thing just to fantasize about him, but to have to see him on the regular, knowing that nothing will ever become of us, just might kill me." Monica thought for a second then commenced to speaking again. "You know what, I take that back. It won't kill me. Seeing him more often and knowing that we will never be just might help me to finally get over him. When is he coming back?" Monica perked up.

"He's been traveling back and forth for the past couple of weeks meeting with realtors and getting set up with his new team for his company here. He'll be here to stay for good in about three months."

"Great. I'll be even stronger in three months. I can do this. I can do all things through Christ that strengthens me." Monica wasn't sure if what she had said about working to get over Keith was entirely true, but she planned to do it.

Afterwards, the ladies finished catching up on each other's lives and then went their separate ways for the evening.

***

Monica knew that she loved Keith from the moment that she met him in high school. He was the only freshman on the varsity basketball team and he was fine. Monica was new to the neighborhood and hadn't made any friends yet. She decided to go to the basketball game one Friday night as opposed to going to church with her mother for the fourth time that week. She walked into the massive gym and immediately became nervous with finding a seat, opting to sit next to three girls who seemed to be harmless and might not tease her about her girth.

She sat quietly, staring at Keith doing his thing on the court during the first half of the game. Half time came and the boys behind Monica began to point and laugh at her. Kim noticed what they were doing and shut them down before Monica was aware of what was going on. Kim introduced herself, Renee, and Pam to Monica. They all became friends.

About a week into their friendship and Monica discreetly stalking Keith, Kim invited Monica over to her house for a sleepover. Monica obliged.

Kim had made Monica aware of the fact that she, Renee, and her brother were triplets, but she never shared who her brother was. Monica was busy scarfing down pizza that Friday evening at the sleepover when Keith stormed in the room and began to hit all of the girls with pillows. There was so much going on that Monica didn't even recognize that it was Keith who had knocked her off her feet yet again, until they all stopped screaming and laughing to make sure that she was alright. Keith leaned over her and extended his hand to help her up. Monica was so embarrassed and nervous that she threw up all over his feet. While Monica cleaned up the mess she made, she admitted to the girls how big of a crush she had on him. They encouraged her to let Keith know that she liked him, but she told them that she wouldn't and swore them to secrecy. As the years went on, Monica's attraction only grew stronger for Keith.

8

Three months later and after a lot of hard work was put in at the gym, Monica weighed in at 215 pounds. It wasn't where she wanted to be, but it definitely wasn't where she used to be.

One day after working out, she showered and rushed to her notebook to jot down the piece racing through her head.

Elegy to Low Self-Esteem

You once had me entangled in your grip
Feeling the shame of my disproportionate hips
Because of my circumstances you snuck up on me
One day making me appear to be someone external
    to me
It wasn't just one thing that caused us to form a
    bond

But rather several incidences that made our courtship last for so long

My mother's strict instruction left me with a religious foundation

A foundation full of knowledge, but at the time, no wisdom to apply the revelations.

So many things conflicting in a child at such a young age were enough to shatter my being

Making me fragile and susceptible to believe even the most negative of comments expressed to me

So I took it to heart when someone called me ugly,

Made fun of me because I was as huge as a hippo,

Poked at me because of how knock-kneed I am,

Or the fact that my toes resemble the length of my hands

In my mind, the unattractive parts of me outweighed the good

So I cleaved to the negative and allowed myself to continue to be verbally degraded

But now that I know myself and understand my worth

I'm mindful of my purpose here on earth

I've severed the ties we had long ago

Renounced every lie you led me to believe about myself

Embraced the beauty both inside and outside of me

That's why I am capable of standing here with you after a long battle in divorce court

The gavel has been pounded and I'm finally free of the union you and I once shared

Monica had truly heeded Renee's advice and went back to her first love—God. She wasn't just working on her outer appearance, more importantly she was working on her inner beauty. She was really beginning to see how beautiful she was from the inside out. It didn't matter to her anymore if men didn't gawk at her, although they had started to do that more lately.

Monica liked who she saw when she looked in the mirror, knowing that she wasn't perfect but was being perfected by the Creator, and she loved it. She read the Bible daily and took comfort in God's promises that He would never leave her nor forsake her, that He would give her the desires of her heart, and that she was fearfully and wonderfully made. She had finally realized that she didn't have to wait on a man to define her; she determined who she was. She walked around confidently with her head held high.

It was a Thursday evening and Monica had decided to treat herself to dinner. She reserved a table for one at a quaint restaurant on Lake Shore Dr. The waiter had just taken her order. She decided to go to the ladies' room before her food arrived. She wore a fitted button-up blouse tucked into a fitted black pencil skirt. The black six-inch stilettos that graced her feet elongated her legs and boosted her sex appeal. Monica bought and wore the outfit simply as a celebration of her weight loss accomplishments, not to impress a man; but that is exactly what she did to Ron as she walked towards his table en route to the bathroom.

"Monica, is that you?" Ron reached out and grabbed Monica's wrist to stop her in her tracks.

Her eyes widened as it registered with her exactly who had stopped her. "Yes, it's me." She pulled away from his hand.

Ron stood. "You look... you look amazing."

"Thanks," Monica said sarcastically and proceeded to walk away, but Ron slightly tugged on her wrist to stay.

"I deserve your attitude. I'm sorry for the way I treated you." Ron couldn't manage to keep his eyes from roaming all over Monica's body. The trainer in him spoke. "You look so toned."

She stepped back from him.

"I know I was a jerk, but if you give me another chance, I promise I will be a better man," Ron pleaded, hoping that he could get in bed with Monica soon.

"No thank you. You weren't the one for me then and I'm certain you aren't the one for me now. I can still see that fake sincerity in your eyes. Goodbye."

Monica proceeded to walk off again, but Ron managed to block her.

Ron leaned in to speak. "Monica, I don't beg women so you should know that I am serious about you. I love the things you used to do. Nobody can do it like you, and I know I was the best you've ever had. You told me so." Ron felt someone tapping on his shoulder and turned around to find his pregnant girlfriend seething with anger as she stood with her hands on her hips. She had heard his pleas for Monica.

Monica looked him up and down before speaking and laughed. "Well, I lied." She smiled as she finally managed to walk away from Ron without him stopping her.

She exited the corridor that housed the restrooms and stopped dead in her tracks again when she noticed another gentleman trying to get her attention.

She slowly approached him. They looked at each other before embracing one another.

"Monica it's so good to see you…come here girl, give me another hug." Keith said in a sultry tenor voice.

Monica didn't know if she could handle the second hug from Keith. He was so strong and his scent was intoxicating. "Keith Williams, how are you doing?"

Monica flashed her winning smile that Keith always loved. She never knew it, but he had a crush on her when they were in high school and in college. Even though he went to a college completely on the other side of the country, he always kept tabs on Monica, hoping to make a relationship work between them. He subdued his crush for her after his sisters had reported to him several times about Monica still not believing in herself. Tonight she was different. He had never seen her exude so much confidence, especially with the way she handled herself with the creep who wouldn't leave her alone until the other woman showed up.

"Why so formal, Mo?" He laughed, referring to her nickname he alone used for her.

"Just kidding with you. So how have you been? I know you've been here for three months and have tried to catch up with me, but I've just been so busy with all the events that I've had to coordinate and my rigid workout schedule. You know these pounds won't shed on their own."

Keith scanned Monica from head to toe. "It's cool. I understand how it is to be busy. And Mo, you look amazing."

Monica's cheeks grew warm.

"Thanks, Keith, I see my waiter is ready to serve my food, so I guess I need to get back to me seat. I'll see you around. Enjoy the rest of your evening."

Monica proceeded to sashay back to her seat, but Keith's voice interrupted her stride.

"Mo, can I join you for dinner?"

She turned around to face him. "You looked as if you were leaving?"

"I had dinner with one of my colleagues. I was preparing to leave until I spotted you talking to that jerk. He seemed creepy, so I decided to stick around and make sure that you were okay. I'll leave you alone if you want me to, but I would love to catch up with you. Reminisce on old times?" Keith hoped that he didn't sound too needy. He really did want to remain in Monica's presence, but he didn't want to make her aware of how attracted he was to her just yet.

Monica assured Keith that it would be fine for him to join her for dinner. He followed her to her table. Seeing as though he had already eaten moments earlier, he ordered dessert.

Monica spoke in between chewing. "Kim said you were moving back to start your family. Are congratulations in order? Are you engaged? Baby on the way?"

"That Kim talks too much." Keith inwardly swore to talk to his sister about her big mouth.

"As always," Monica said and they both laughed.

"No, I'm not engaged. I'm not even in a relationship, so there's definitely no baby on the way. My company opened up a new office here that I'm heading up. I decided to accept the management position and make the move because while I did enjoy California after I graduated, my heart has always been in Chicago."

"Why? It's so cold here in the winters."

They both laughed again.

"As Kim told you, I moved for my job, and more importantly family. I get to consistently be around my mother and father, whom I love dearly. I can now get back to being the protector for my sisters and their friend, Pam, and especially you."

Monica sat blushing at Keith's last comment but quickly dismissed his protectiveness of her as just brotherly gestures. "That's so sweet, Keith. I always considered you to be like a brother to me." Monica didn't know where that lie had come from, but she decided to stick with it. Although she appreciated Keith dining with her that evening and the compliments he was showering on her, she figured that was all a formality due to not having seen her in such a long time.

Keith wasn't sure how to take Monica's statement. He never wanted to be her brother, not when they were younger and certainly not now. Staring at the confident woman she had become energized the feelings he had for her. In due time, he would share with her how he truly felt.

Monica and Keith continued to catch up with one another. They vowed to keep in touch before they parted ways for the evening.

9

Three months had managed to go by since Monica had seen Keith. They spoke on the phone as often as they could, but she truly was engulfed with her alone time with God, her work, and her workouts. Her newly found confidence had landed her even more events to coordinate. She was saddened by the fact that she hadn't seen her best friends in months, but her workload called for her to host events while the ladies were at the Mellow Lounge on Friday nights and also when they were at brunch on Sunday afternoons.

That was the case this Friday night. It was one o'clock in the morning and Monica had just returned home from hosting an event for Chicago's Fire Department. Although she missed hanging out with her girls again that night, she relished in the fact of coming home alone and not being disheartened about it. She had become very satisfied with the quality time she spent with God and herself. She was grateful to be alone because she knew that her newly found patience in waiting on God to send her a man would be worth the wait. She thanked God for every man that He didn't allow to stay in her life, even her father. Even though it was a long road to self-discovery, she appreciated the lessons she had learned from the absent men in her life; she didn't need to depend on a man for happiness. She could rely on God to give her unlimited joy.

She lit chamomile scented candles and filled her soaking tub with bath beads. She just wanted to relax. She found the Sade station on Pandora and let Sade's smooth, mellow voice fill her dimly lit bathroom. Monica relaxed and soaked in the tub until the water became lukewarm. Then, she got out and prepared herself to go to bed.

***

Monica woke up refreshed the next morning. She made a protein shake to drink before she went to work out. She couldn't help but miss her friends. She hated not being able to attend yet another brunch with them the following day when it dawned on her that she could just invite them to the event that she was hosting that Sunday. She decided to send out a mass text: *Hey, ladies! I miss you all so much. I know this is short notice, but since I can't meet you all for brunch tomorrow, how about we shake things up and you all attend my charity event tomorrow? It'll give you all a chance to get all dolled up. LOL. I hope that you all can make it. It's at 5 p.m. @...*

The ladies had all responded to Monica by the time she arrived at the gym, confirming that they indeed would attend. She was excited about seeing her friends as she gave her Saturday morning workout all that she had. Monica ended her workout about two hours later. She stopped by the grocery store to grab some produce. She headed home and spent the rest of the day lounging and finalizing plans for the event the next day.

***

Once again, Monica worked the crowd while her friends stood by and admired how confident and sexy she looked. Monica looked even slimmer than the last time they saw her. She'd just finished chatting with the chief of firefighters when she spotted her friends amidst the crowd. "Ladies, I'm so happy that you all could make it. I've missed you all so much," Monica exclaimed as she hugged and air kissed each one of them.

"Where did Monica go? Who is this woman in front of me? She has Monica's face, but certainly not her confidence," Kim joked with Monica.

"I know, right. This is definitely not the old Monica," Monica said as she framed her new silhouette with her hands. "I'm definitely not the same on the inside either. I'm happy with myself now. Loving the skin that I'm in."

"We loved the old Monica just as much, but this new Monica, there's a fierceness about her," Pam said and snapped her fingers simultaneously.

"And what do you have to say, Renee?" Monica laughed.

Renee grabbed Monica's hand. "Nothing, other than you look fabulous. I'm so happy you realized your inner beauty. You're radiating healthy confidence now."

"I'm still staring at your outer appearance. How much weight have you lost since the last time we saw you, girl?" Kim scanned Monica's physique.

"Well I've lost twenty-five pounds since the last time I saw you all, so now I weigh 190 pounds compared to me weighing 270 pounds, soon to be a year ago." Monica's smile spread wide.

"I am so proud of you, Monica. We all are. Not to take the spotlight off of you now because you do deserve it, but please help me to understand exactly why there are so many fine men up in here!" Kim said, fanning herself, pretending to faint.

Monica giggled. "Oh, did I forget to mention that this charity event for the fire department is an auction of eligible bachelors in the Chicagoland area? I figured what better way for us to enjoy ourselves than to be around fine men. While I'm not looking to date right now, it sure doesn't hurt to look." Monica fanned herself, looking over her shoulder as a bachelor walked past her. "I can't take the credit for coming up with the auction. The men had it planned out to be auctioned off for dates to raise funds for the department. It's just my job to make sure that the night goes by without a hiccup."

"So, Monica, are you bidding on someone tonight? I just might." Kim licked her lips.

"Cut it out, Kim." Monica laughed. "No, I'm not. I'm enjoying being single."

Kim, Pam, and Renee stood quietly with smirks on their faces.

"Why are you all looking at me like that? What, you don't believe me?"

"So is that why you've been avoiding me all this time?" A deep, sultry voice whispered in Monica's ear.

Monica didn't have to turn around to know who it was. She smelled the intoxicating scent of his cologne. The sexy tenor in his voice made her heart flutter. She knew it was Keith. "I'm going to get you all." She mouthed to the ladies before turning to face Keith.

Kim, Pam, and Renee all giggled.

"Keith, what a surprise." Monica accepted Keith's outstretched arms for a hug. She felt at home in his embrace but quickly broke away, resolving that they would never be.

She looked down at the fluffy corsage he held in his hand. Her forehead creased. "For me?"

"Of course." He winked at her.

"Thanks, it's beautiful and just like the one you gave me the night of our prom." Monica felt the sparks of electricity flying between her and Keith and felt it was best if she left. She had to continue to ignore her feelings for him. "I'm sorry you all, I have to go and check on some things. See ya soon."

"We told you that we would be here but we didn't know that you would come," Renee said to her brother.

"What? I'm an eligible bachelor in the Chicagoland area. Can't I be a part of the auction?" Keith laughed and ushered the ladies to their seats as they were being called to do so.

Monica intentionally avoided going over to the ladies table that night since Keith was sitting with them.

The group spotted Monica as they exited the coat room at the end of the evening as she wished the guests a good night.

"Monica, we wished you would've come to the table with us for a while. You just seemed to stand off in corners of the room for quite some time by yourself," Pam said.

Keith bore holes into Monica with his eyes. "I, uh, um…I had to be stationed at those particular places. You remember I was hosting tonight, right?" she said jokingly, hoping to assuage her friends from worrying about her.

"If you say so. I guess since we can't hang out on the weekends then we'll all have to coordinate our schedules for a weekday meet up," Kim said, looking forward to getting together with her friends again. "Toodles. Come on, Keith, walk us to our cars," Kim commanded as she swatted Keith with her clutch purse.

"Just a minute. I need to speak with Monica. I'll meet you all in the main lobby." Keith waited for the ladies to walk off before he spoke to Monica. "Are you really trying to ignore me?"

"Why would you ask that?" Monica patted her bangs, feigning ignorance.

"For the past few weeks I've been calling and texting you. You've either cut our phone calls and text conversations extremely short or you just haven't answered my calls at all. What's up?"

"I can't get into this now." Monica signaled the cleanup crew to begin clearing the tables.

"Well, when can you?" Keith said as he stood behind Monica with his hands on her hips leaning in to her to whisper in her ear.

"Soon, but not now." Monica shivered at his touch as she continued to wave and smile at people as they exited the ballroom.

"Soon, like meeting for coffee after you're done here, soon?"

"Okay. If it'll send you away quicker, yes, I'll meet you for coffee as soon as I'm done here. Just text me where to meet you, but it might be another hour before I'm ready to leave here." Monica hoped that she wasn't making a mistake agreeing to meet Keith for coffee that evening. She didn't know how much longer she could go on lying to herself and him about how she really felt.

Monica directed her staff as they completed their exit strategy for the event. About an hour later she gathered her belongings and left.

***

Monica entered the coffee shop. Keith stared at her. She seemed even more beautiful every time he saw her. He hoped to get more personal with her that night than what he had managed to in the past three months.

Monica couldn't seem to stop her heart from fluttering as she approached the booth Keith was sitting in. He stood when she came closer to the table. They sat down together. The waiter came up and took their orders. Monica ordered jasmine tea while Keith ordered a salted caramel mocha. The waiter left to fill their order.

"Thanks for meeting me." Keith stared into Monica's eyes.

"You're welcome. I would've agreed to meet with you later on this week and we could've went to dinner and had more time to hang out, but you insisted on meeting now. It's already 10:30 at night. I don't know how much longer my eyelids will hold up." Monica laughed, trying to ease the butterflies doing somersaults in her stomach.

"No you wouldn't have." Keith smiled. "You would have agreed to but then would've come up with a reason why you couldn't have dinner with me. Why do you keep blowing me off?"

Monica held a pensive stare.

Keith couldn't read her countenance so he just kept talking. "I've spent the last three months trying to tell you how I feel but you haven't given me the time of day to do so." Keith reached out and grabbed Monica's hand. "I'll get straight to the point. Monica, I care about you. I always have."

Monica paused, in shock, before she spoke. The waiter returned and placed their drinks before each of them. She was trying to decide how to take what

Keith said. "Are you talking about you care for me in a platonic or a romantic way?"

"My attraction to you has never been platonic. I've cared for you since the day I knocked you out with that pillow." They both laughed.

"You sure had a funny way of showing it then." Monica rolled her eyes.

"You've just never noticed it. I've always had feelings for you. Why do you think I took you to our senior prom?"

"Because you felt sorry for me. Kim, Pam, and Renee had boyfriends at the time. I was all alone so you pitied me."

"I never saw you the way you used to see yourself."

"You didn't?"

"But having a mother like I did and two sisters like Kim and Renee, I learned early on that if a girl wasn't happy with herself then nobody could make her happy. I didn't want to ruin our friendship so I just played it off as best as I could as if I wasn't interested in you."

"Well, you did a great job at that," Monica said as she rolled her eyes.

Keith laughed. "To you it may not have seemed as if I cared, but I always have. You just don't know how many fights I got into in the locker rooms in high school taking up for you when those idiot jocks made fun of you. I was ready to come up to Howard and beat that jerk Eric to a pulp because of the way he disrespected you, but Kim talked me out of it. Honestly, you're the biggest reason I moved back to Chicago."

Monica's eyes widened. She placed her hand over her chest as if to calm her rapid heartbeats. "So what does all of this mean?"

"I want a future with you, Monica." Keith grabbed both of her hands into his and looked lovingly into her eyes.

Monica's misty eyes stared back into his. "I've waited so long to hear you say this to me." They held hands and talked nonstop before they decided to call it a night, agreeing to take things slow.

10

Monica and Keith found themselves spending a lot of their free time together, which brought them to the movies that night. They stood in the concession line waiting to get snacks for the suspense movie they were about to see.

"Sir, may I take your order?"

"Yes, I would like a large popcorn with extra butter, some M&M's with peanuts, and two large Sprites."

Monica tapped Keith on his shoulder. "We just had dinner an hour and a half ago, but I take it that you're ready for seconds?" She snickered.

"I'm not necessarily hungry, but we'll have the snacks to munch on during the movie." Keith attempted to give the cashier his American Express card, but Monica stopped him.

"Well just order enough for you. I don't eat this late at night and if I did it certainly wouldn't be buttery popcorn, M&M's, and pop."

"Monica, it's okay to treat yourself every now and then. With the way you work out, the pounds won't stand a chance to stick to you." Keith attempted to hand the card to the cashier again, but the attempt was thwarted, yet again, by Monica.

"I'm sorry, Robert," Monica stared at the cashier's nametag, "but can you make that a small popcorn, M&M's," Monica raised her eyes at Keith and he nodded yes, "a medium sprite, and a bottled water? Thank you." Monica stepped back and finally let Keith give Robert his credit card.

"What a lady you have there." Robert laughed as he handed Keith the card back.

Keith grabbed the items from the counter, and then he and Monica walked toward theater number seven. "Monica, I love the way you look now, but I always have. You're beautiful to me no matter what size you are."

"Thanks, but Keith, eating healthy is a lifestyle for me, not just a way to keep the pounds off. I am very conscious about what I consume now."

"Okay, Mo."

They sat in the upper middle section of the theater. Halfway through the movie and after the small tub of popcorn had been eaten, Keith stretched, and in doing so, draped his arm around Monica.

Monica still couldn't wrap her mind around being with Keith. Her dream had finally come true and sitting there with his arm around her gave her chills. The scent of his cologne was intoxicating to her as usual. The loud noises and graphic images of the car chase on the screen ended horribly, causing Monica to cover her eyes with her hands and lean in to Keith to shield her from seeing the outcome for the victims. He pulled her closer to him and kissed the top of her head.

"You know it's a movie, right? The people aren't really hurt or dead." Keith chuckled.

Monica looked up at him. "I know that silly, it just seems so real and that was a really bad accident." She remained in the crevice of his underarm. Keith interlocked his free hand with hers for the remainder of the show.

"Did you enjoy the movie?" Keith asked as he pulled out of the movie theater's parking lot.

"I sure did, minus all the violence." Monica smiled.

"Aw, all the shooting and the car crashes, those were the best parts." Keith chortled. He drove in silence for a while before he spoke again. "So what will we do for our next date?"

"I thought we agreed to take things slow?" Monica stared out the window.

"Yeah we did, but I thought that meant when it comes to putting a title on what we have or rushing into sex. I think that in order for us to get to know one another better, we have to spend as much time together as possible. Don't you?"

Smiling, Monica turned towards Keith. "Yes, Keith. Spending time together, getting to know one another more is important to me. I just don't want to get comfortable with you or in the habit of being with you and then we don't work out and I'll be left to deal with those emotions."

Keith pulled into Monica's driveway and turned the car off. He shifted in his seat to look directly at her, his intense stare going unnoticed as she looked ahead into a rose bush. He gently grabbed her chin and tilted her head towards him. "Monica?"

"Yes," she whispered.

"I have no intentions of us ending. I agreed to take things slow with you, but know that I'm all in this. My feelings for you are sincere." He gently rubbed the side of her face and grabbed her hand to kiss it.

"Okay." She smirked.

He got out of the car and went around to open her door. They walked to the front door. "Thanks for tonight, I really enjoyed myself." Monica blushed.

"No problem. The pleasure was all mine." Keith pushed back strands of hair from Monica's face.

"Goodnight. Talk to you soon." Monica turned to unlock her door, but Keith pulled her into a comforting embrace. He held her in his arms for a while before letting her go. She unlocked the door and stepped into the house. "Let me know when you make it home." She smiled.

"Okay. Goodnight." Keith walked away only after hearing Monica lock the door from the inside.

I made it home. Monica received the text from Keith and was finally able to go to sleep knowing that he had made it home safely.

***

Monica and Keith talked and text daily over the next few weeks. They went out on dates at least two nights of the week, growing closer and closer.

"Mo, are you almost ready?" Keith yelled to Monica as he sat on her couch.

"I'm trying to be, but I could go faster if you stop asking me that every minute." Monica giggled as she stepped out of her master closet and back into her bathroom, wearing only a black lace matching bra and panty set. "I'm putting on my makeup now."

"You don't need makeup on. You're such a natural beauty." Keith shook his head thinking how long it took some women to get ready. Monica was one of them. He did admit to himself that she always looked good whenever he saw her. She was worth the wait. He surfed through channels looking for something to watch.

"Thanks. I don't wear much, just eye shadow and mascara." She had just finished applying the mascara to her eyelashes when she inhaled the scent of him. She turned to her left to look at him. He was leaning against the doorway staring intensely at her. He held her gaze. "Keith why are you in here? I'm not even fully dressed yet." Her throat seemed dry all of a sudden.

"I see that." He smirked, able to see her sensual curves in the flesh. "I'm sorry for just coming in here unannounced, but I was trying to see if I could assist you in getting dressed so we won't be late." He looked down at his watch to avert his attention from her body.

She quickly backed up into the closet. "Keith, get out of here! I'll be out in a minute. I just need to put my dress and shoes on. I am going to get you for just walking in on me like this." Monica beamed, thinking about how pleased Keith seemed to be with what he saw. She knew that physical attraction and looks weren't everything but it felt nice to her for Keith to really admire how she looked.

"Whatever you do will be worth it; I enjoyed the view." He chuckled as he walked back to the living room.

Monica came into the living room in a black fitted sleeveless dress that fell just above her knees. She twirled. "I'm ready."

"Yes, and it only took you two hours. You're getting better with time." Keith chuckled as he came from around the front of the couch to be face to face with Monica.

"Don't you ever walk in on me like that again." Monica playfully punched Keith on the arm.

He pulled her into him and rested his arms on the small of her back, staring into her eyes. "I'm sorry." He poked his lips out with a puppy dog face.

Monica leaned in to him. "I forgive you." She gave him a peck on his lips. He tried to go in for a deeper kiss, but she pulled away, wagging her finger in the air.

"No, no, no. Remember you were rushing me so that we can get there on time. We don't have time for a make-out session." She pulled away from him and headed towards the front door. Keith followed after her.

"Yes, we do." He laughed. "We can be late if it means that I get to kiss you." He stood behind her, kissing her on her neck as she struggled to put her jacket on.

"Let's go, Keith." She turned to him, kissed him on the lips, and then pulled him out of the door.

They arrived at the lounge half an hour later. It was a Chicago Stepper's set and after having taken a few classes together, they were ready to show what they learned. The smooth music flowing from the DJ's booth primed them to get on the dance floor. The steps in the dance kept them moving in opposing directions at half an arm's length between the two of them, but that didn't stop the heat emanating between them. After dancing through six songs, nonstop, they decided to go back to their seats.

"Whew! That was fun."

"Yeah it was," Keith responded.

"We looked good out there. You would think that we've been doing this for years," Monica said as she fanned herself to cool off.

"What, dancing or liking each other?" Keith stared intently at Monica.

"Why must you always flirt with me?" Monica felt her temperature rising even more.

"Not flirting. Just always in the mood to share how I feel about you."

"Oh." Monica's hand moved more rapidly in the fanning motion.

"You don't have to be nervous around me." Keith smirked.

"Not nervous, just hot from dancing," she lied.

"If you say so." He laughed. "Wanna order something to eat or drink?"

"Not hungry. I do want some cranberry juice though."

Keith signaled a waitress and placed their drink order. They drank and then danced through eight more songs before they called it a night.

Smooth jazz filling the car as Keith caressed her hand. She was tired, and within minutes into the ride home, she fell asleep.

"Mo, wake up. You're home." He gently squeezed her hand.

"Hmm?" She woke up disoriented. "I fell asleep on you? I'm sorry, I didn't mean to do that. I was just so comfortable with you, I just dozed off." She sat up.

"You don't have to explain anything. I know that you have had a lot of events to plan and I've been taking up a lot of your free time."

"That's not a bad thing. You haven't been taking up space, you've been filling it." Monica smiled at him.

"Now who's flirting?" Keith laughed and got out of the car to walk around and open her door.

"You are so silly." Monica smiled slyly. They walked hand in hand to the front door. "I really enjoyed dancing with you tonight."

"Yeah, I just wish we would've gone to a jazz club, then we could've slow danced and I would've been all up on you." Keith pulled her into him and swayed from side to side. She matched his rhythm.

"We have plenty of time to slow dance." Monica stood on her tip toes to kiss Keith. He gripped her tighter as he explored her mouth and tried to share how he felt about her through their kiss. When the kiss ended Monica had to brace herself against him to regain her composure. She backed up from him and stared into his eyes. Nothing was said, but everything was understood. "Goodnight, Keith." She pivoted towards the door and unlocked it.

"Goodnight, Bae. I'll text you and let you know when I make it home."

Monica's eyebrows raised as she stared at Keith. "Bae?"

"Yeah, you're my baby, my Bae." Keith smiled as he walked back to his car.

Monica entered the house, locked the door, and fell back against the door with a huge grin on her face. *I'm his bae?* She squealed as she set the alarm then glided to her bedroom.

11

"So what are you up to tonight, Bae?" Keith asked Monica, hoping to be able to spend some time with her.

"Well, once I wrap up the details for Sunday's event I'm going to have dinner with the girls."

"Oh."

Monica could detect the sadness in his voice. "Keith, one night apart from each other won't hurt us." She laughed. "You know they say absence makes the heart grow fonder." Monica cooed.

"I can't imagine getting anymore fonder of you than I already am. I mean, how much more can a man love a woman than I do you?"

"What did you just say?" Monica was nervous he would take back or change what he said.

"What, that I love you?"

"Keith, don't play with my feelings."

"Monica, I've loved you for a long time. The time we've spent together the last couple of months has only confirmed and matured my love for you."

Monica became misty eyed. "Keith?"

"Yes."

"If you were here right now I would hit you."

Keith laughed. "Now why would you do that?"

"I've waited for so long to hear you say those words to me and you tell me over the phone." Monica pouted.

"Let me come over and I'll tell you to your face."

"I already told you that I have plans with the girls tonight. You can say it to my face tomorrow night and I'll pretend like it's the first time I'm hearing it, tears and all."

"You're silly. Let me let you get back to what you were doing. Call me when you get in tonight. I love you."

She was too enamored with his admission to even say it back to him. Her smile seemed to stretch from ear to ear as she hung up the phone.

***

"This is so much better now that we're not trying to meet on the weekends anymore. All four of us get to hang out on a more consistent basis and now I don't have to stop turning down so many men begging for a date with me." Kim laughed as they sat at the table at the Mexican restaurant waiting for their orders to be filled.

"Whatever, Kim," Monica said and all of the ladies broke out in laughter.

"So how have you been treating my brother? How has he been treating you?" Renee looked at Monica.

"Just great. You know I had become happy with being single before he and I got together. Not wanting to go back to my old dependent ways, I've been trying to take it slow and keep my emotions at bay, but Keith is really making that hard for me."

"How so?" Pam asked.

"Well he's so kind and gentle. He's really attentive," Monica squealed. "Tonight, he told me that he loved me."

"You say that like that's something new," Kim said. Renee and Pam joined her in laughter.

"What?" Monica's eyebrows furrowed.

"Monica, sorry we've kept it from you. We've known for a long time that he's loved you. He just swore us to secrecy." Pam spoke up.

"So you all have let me agonize over him not liking me while you all have known how he has truly felt?" Monica was truly hurt.

The ladies saw Monica's countenance change and they rushed to find words to appease her.

"We're sorry but we just couldn't tell you. Yes, Keith has loved you for a long time, but Monica, he was wise enough to know that he couldn't have a successful and meaningful relationship with a woman who didn't love herself. So he's kept tabs on you all these years, knowing that you would learn your worth soon enough and then he would pursue you if you allowed him," Kim said.

"Yeah, we're sorry for keeping this from you, but we knew that you two could have something beautiful at the right time and we just didn't want that to be ruined. Shoot, we didn't want you with any man until you truly loved yourself," Renee confessed.

Monica paused before speaking. "Although I don't like it, I guess I understand why you all have kept this from me. I've really wanted him all these years because I thought that he could make me happy, but I'm glad we didn't get together until I understood where my joy comes from, God." Monica began to cry. "When I first started this weight loss journey, this time around, I was doing it so that I could get slim and maybe get a man, but it evolved into something bigger." She smiled. "The more I changed my eating habits, you know, getting rid of the toxic food that I loved so much, the more I realized that the journey was about changing my desires to crave things and food that could lead to a long, healthy life. Before, I allowed my emotions to dictate what food and how much of it I ate, but now, if I feel a certain way I really explore my feelings and issues to understand and resolve them the right way. Not just bury them in food. Food was my vice but for others it may be sex, drugs, alcohol, or whatever else that may temporarily take their minds off of their problems. I'm so glad that I have friends like you all that didn't allow me to just throw my life away with my low self-esteem. By encouraging me to lose weight, because you all knew that's what I wanted to do, you actually pushed me to find myself. I love you all."

They all stood and hugged Monica and cried with her.

"We love you too, Monica, but can you stop all this mushy stuff? You'll ruin my makeup." Kim always managed to bring moments back to her looks.

Monica's phone alerted her of a text message. "Keith knows that I am out with you all and yet he's texting me now." Monica smiled at the messages she was receiving from him.

"While I have enjoyed myself, ladies, it's getting late and I need to get home to get ready for work tomorrow." Renee informed them.

"Me, too. I had a long day today and an even longer day at work tomorrow." Pam yawned.

The ladies gave each other hugs and kisses before they went to their cars and went their separate ways.

***

"Hey. I made it home, Keith," Monica said into the phone.

"Okay, beautiful. See you tomorrow night, right?" Keith had been waiting to hear from her.

"Yes, Keith, we're still on for dinner tomorrow night."

"Okay, goodnight, my love."

"Goodnight, Keith." Monica crooned.

***

Monica awoke the next morning charged to complete her daily workout. She burned more calories than she had expected to, which made her even more happy that day. She returned home, showered, and began fleshing out the details for her next event. It was going to be a masquerade ball for the Chicago's Nurse's Association. She had spent hours working on the plans for the masquerade before she dozed off and was awakened by a text message alert from Keith.

Pick you up around 6 tonight ;)

Monica looked at the time on her cell phone and realized that it was already 5pm. She rushed to her room, showered, dressed, styled her hair, and applied her makeup. She was just putting the finishing touches on her makeup when her doorbell rang.

"Hey, beautiful." Keith hugged her.

"Hi, honey." She relaxed in Keith's arms and they shared a brief, yet passionate, kiss. She set the alarm before closing the door as they headed to his car. Like the gentleman that he was, Keith opened the passenger door for Monica and waited until she was buckled up before he closed the door. Once secure in his seat belt, he looked in the rearview mirror of his coupe Benz and backed out of the driveway, headed towards the restaurant.

***

As soon as the waiter took their orders and left the table, Keith didn't hesitate to compliment Monica.

"You manage to look even more beautiful every time I see you."

"Oh stop it, Keith. You're going to make my cheeks hurt from blushing and smiling so much. You've always had that effect on me."

"I bet we're going to have beautiful kids together. I hope our daughter looks just like you with those beautiful, hazel eyes and that smooth, mocha skin." Keith reached out and traced circles on Monica's forearm.

Monica became nervous at the mention of kids. She shifted in her seat. The waiter placed their food on the table. They bowed their heads and Keith blessed the food.

"Are you okay?" Keith noticed Monica becoming uneasy in his presence.

"Yeah everything is fine. I just got a hot flash or something." Monica sipped on her water.

Keith reached across the table and interlaced his hands with Monica's. "So how many kids do you want?"

"We haven't even talked marriage yet and you're all excited about kids."

Keith stared into Monica's eyes. "Monica, I do want to marry you."

Monica relished Keith's acknowledgement that he wanted to marry her; she just couldn't help but to be nervous about his talk of children. She chewed slowly on her food to avoid having to talk.

"So, now that I've made that clear, you can answer my question. How many kids do you see us having?"

"Um, uh, excuse me but I really have to go to the bathroom." Monica scurried from the table and ran to hide in the bathroom. She had taken her purse with her so she had her cell phone to call Kim.

"Kim!"

"Monica, I'm kinda busy now, what do you want?" Kim whispered as she beckoned for her male friend to stop nibbling on her ear.

"I really need to talk to you now. Wait, who is that I hear in the background? Is there a man at your house?"

"Mind your business. You called me to talk about you, not me. What do you want?" Kim giggled.

"It's Keith. He keeps bringing up kids. Kim, I haven't told him that I can't have kids. I love him so much and I don't want to lose what we have, but I know he won't still want me if I can't bear any children for him. No man will." Monica wiped the tears that began to cover her face.

"Monica. It's okay. Keith is sensible. He'll understand. You two can always adopt. I believe his love for you outweighs anything else."

"But, Kim, you didn't see the way he looked at me, thinking I would be the mother of his children."

"I'm telling you, girl, just be honest with him and everything will work out just fine. Don't get so worked up over this. It's not as bad as you think it is. You know I love you, but I have to go now. As you heard, I have company…stop Derrick, you're so silly." Kim's escapades could be heard before she hung up the phone.

Monica knew that she should be honest with Keith but she just couldn't bring herself to do so. She left the stall. At the mirror, she touched up her makeup, plastered a smile on her face and exited the bathroom.

Keith stood as Monica approached their table. "Mo, are you okay? Have you been crying?"

"Oh, I'm okay. You know what, Keith, I'm really tired. I'm ready to call it a night."

"We haven't been here that long. You've barely touched your food."

"I'm not really hungry."

"Is it something you're not telling me? Your mood changed so quickly when I started talking about marriage. Is that what it is? You don't want to marry me?"

"Keith…That's all I've wanted to do since the day I met you. I love you. I want to spend the rest of my life with you, I'm just honestly tired right now and ready to go home. Will you take me please?"

Keith signaled for the waiter to come to the table with the check. Once the waiter returned with the receipt, Keith signed it, left a tip, and escorted Monica to the car.

The ride to Monica's house was silent. When Keith reached for her hand, he felt her tremble so he drew back. The more he thought about it he figured that maybe if he showed Monica just how serious he was about her, the more comfortable she would be with the thought of marrying him. He pulled up to her house and walked her to the door. He stared into her eyes, inching slowly to her face and softly brushing his lips against hers. He pulled her closer to him. He rubbed the small of her back as his tongue parted her lips and intertwined with hers. They swayed, kissing in the moonlight until Monica pulled back from him. She hugged him longingly before going in the house. She wanted to feel what it would be like to be in his arms one last time.

Unlike Keith, she was thinking that she would have to end their relationship before he found out about her infertility.

***

"Kim, what's up with Monica?"

"And hello to you too! What do you mean, Keith?"

"We were all lovey-dovey one minute, last night, and then the moment I started talking about us getting married and having kids she went numb on me, like she saw a ghost or something."

Kim didn't know how to respond. She never lied to her brother and wondered if he could detect if she did; but she couln't betray Monica's trust by telling him the truth behind Monica's behavior. "Don't read too much into that. Maybe she just felt ill all of sudden. Did you ask her about it?"

"Yes and she denied that it was anything wrong with us, just that she was tired and needed to get home to rest."

"Well then, there's your answer."

"Okay, I'll let it go for now. I won't push because I know that she's probably sworn you to some type of secrecy, but if she acts like that again around me then someone is going to have to tell me the real truth."

"Boy, you don't scare me." Kim laughed.

"How about helping me plan a surprise birthday party for Monica?"

"Sure. I think that would be great."

"The best part about that night is that I'm going to propose to her."

"Oh my God, Keith! You are?"

"Yeah, lil' sister. I am."

"I'm only your little sister by two minutes, so don't go there." Kim and Keith laughed. "So, do you have a ring, or do you need my expertise with picking out one?"

"I already have it. I've had it for about two months now."

"You really are serious about Monica?"

"Kim, you of all people know how much and for how long I've loved her. Maybe once I propose to her she'll see how serious I am about us. I just can't shake how uneasy she was when I was talking about our future last night."

"Don't worry about that. I'm pretty sure once you propose to her she'll see how dedicated you are to her then. Everything will be fine for the two of you. Do you have any ideas of how you plan to propose?"

Kim and Keith continued to talk until they had planned the party for Monica that would take place in two weeks.

***

"Why do you have me blindfolded, Keith?"

"Obviously it's a surprise, baby. Step up. Okay, we're going to your right. Stop trying to peak from under the blindfold." Keith laughed as he directed Monica to where the surprise party was taking place. He entered the room and signaled for the band to play the music.

"Surprise!" Everyone screamed in unison as Keith took off Monica's blindfold. The band started playing Stevie Wonder's, *Happy Birthday*.

"Ohhhh." A wide grin spread across Monica's face as her eyes gleamed with excitement of what Keith had done for her. She pinched herself to make sure the bliss she was experiencing was real before partygoers beckoned her to them.

Keith was on her heels as she walked the room greeting the guests.

Kim, Pam, and Renee were there as well as some of their high school friends that they kept in touch with. Monica's mother was there along with Keith's parents. Many of Monica's clients whom she had close relationships with were there to wish her a happy birthday and take in the peaceful neo-soul atmosphere, dim lights, and the smooth sounds played by the band.

They had made a full circle around the room before Monica turned around to Keith on her heels.

She pulled him over into a corner and looked into his eyes. "Keith, this is all so beautiful." Monica pointed at the beautiful rustic décor of the venue. "I can't believe you did all this for me. Thank you. I know that the night has just begun but you've made it so very special thus far. I've never had a birthday like this, my thirtieth birthday with the love of my life and all of my friends and my mother here to share in this day with me. Thank you, honey."

"You're welcome, baby. I love you so much. I just want you to enjoy tonight and all that it has to offer."

Keith led Monica to the dance floor and held her tightly as they slow-danced. By the time the song was done, Keith had secretly signaled for the band to begin to play his next request, *At Last* by Etta James. Kim had motioned all of the other couples dancing to clear the floor. The only two that were left on the floor were Keith and Monica. Keith danced for a second with Monica to the song before he requested that she sit in the seat that Kim had brought to the middle of the dance floor. A spotlight beamed on them. The music lowered upon Keith's request. He stood over Monica and stared into her eyes.

"Monica Michelle Sutton. I've loved you since the day I met you. I've prayed for you for so long. I've been one of your biggest fans. I know that you're the woman for me. My best friend for life. The woman that I am to marry. The mother of my future children." Keith sank to one knee, holding Monica's hand. Monica cried. "Baby will you do me the honor of being my wife?"

All eyes were on Monica. The phrase "the mother of my children" just kept playing in her head. She had wanted this moment with Keith for so long. "Keith. I love you so much. You have no idea how much I really love you." Monica struggled to speak through her tears.

"Just say yes, baby," Keith pleaded.

"I love you so much, but I just can't..." Monica fled hysterically from the restaurant.

12

Everyone in the room was in shock. They began to whisper, speculating why Monica said no. Keith was still on bended knee, shocked as he came to his senses and decided to chase after Monica. He ran out of the venue and caught up with her about a block from the restaurant. He had to run around in front of her to get her to stop. She stopped running, but her tears continued to flow.

He caught his breath before he said, "Monica, I don't get it. You say you love me but you don't want to marry me?"

Monica paused as long as she could but saw that his sad eyes deserved an answer. "Keith, you just don't how much it hurts me that we can't be together. I can't give you what you want."

"Yes, you can, baby. All I want is you. We'll start a family soon enough, but now, I want you." Keith stroked Monica's face.

She jerked away from him. "That's it! You don't want me because I can't give you a family, Keith. I can't have kids. I'll never be able to have your son or your daughter." Monica ran off.

Keith stood still in shock.

She ran until she couldn't run anymore. And then, she hailed a cab.

"Where to, Miss?"

"I don't know, just drive," Monica said absentmindedly.

"Are you okay?"

"Yes, I'm fine. I don't want to talk. Please, just drive." Monica was exhausted from crying.

"Okay, but the meter will run." The driver smiled.

"I know, just DRIVE!"

Twenty minutes into the ride she gave the driver directions to her house.

Keith was already waiting on her doorstep when she got there.

"Keith, I can't do this tonight." Monica opened her front door, hoping to leave Keith on the outside of it.

"Monica, you can't just say what you said to me and we not talk about it."

"What is there to talk about? I know you love me but I can see in your eyes how much you want kids, too. I can't give them to you, Keith. I don't want to marry you only for you to resent me down the line for not giving you the life that you want. I want you to be happy, and if you can get that happiness from another woman then I want you to." Monica tried to close the door, but Keith put his foot in it and welcomed himself into her house. She was emotionally drained. She retired to the couch in her living room. So did he.

"Monica. Yes, I want kids, but more importantly I want you. Who told you that you couldn't have kids anyway?"

Monica was tired of keeping the truth from him so she decided to tell him everything. "Keith, I did something stupid in college. My self-esteem was so low back then that I had sex with any man that gave me attention. Since it wasn't that many, I found comfort in a reoccurring one. His name was Paul. We used protection the first couple of times we did it and then one day he told me he wanted to see what I felt like. I knew he didn't love me and we weren't an official couple but I didn't want to lose him, so I agreed. A month later, I found out that I was pregnant. I told him and he told me that I better go and find the baby's daddy. I was so humiliated. I knew my mother would be so disappointed in me because she didn't raise me to be so loose and carefree. The more I thought about what to do, the more I thought about how my father was never around for me and the effects it had on me. I didn't want that for my child, so I thought the only thing I could do was to get an abortion. I knew it wasn't right, but I decided to anyway. When I went back for a checkup months later, after the procedure, the doctors discovered that an infection had occurred during the abortion, not to mention severe uterine and cervical lacerations, which ended up making me sterile. I accepted it as my punishment for destroying a life." Monica put her head in her hands and cried. Keith rubbed her back before pulling her into his embrace. She leaned into him and cried on his chest.

"Monica, I'm sorry you had to go through that, but baby, that doesn't change the way I feel about you. So what, we can't have biological kids. We can always adopt."

"You don't mean that." Monica pulled away from Keith.

"Yes, I do." He lifted her chin and turned her head towards him. He stared intently into her eyes.

Monica searched Keith's eyes and saw sincerity in what he was saying.

"Yes, I do. I just want to be with you."

"So, you still want to marry me?"

"Of course, and as soon as possible." Keith smiled and pulled Monica into a tender kiss.

They sat quietly in each other's arms before Keith kissed Monica good night and left.

13

Monica and Keith didn't waste any time setting a date for their wedding after he proposed to her.

"How can you plan a wedding for two weeks from now?" Kim asked in amazement.

"Well luckily, I know some people who owe me some favors." Monica laughed. "I don't want a big elaborate wedding. I'm marrying the man of my dreams and that's enough for me. I want the wedding to be intimate, simple, yet elegant."

"You're such a great event planner, I bet you'll get just that. Is there anything you need for us to do?" Renee asked.

"Just to get your dresses since you all will be my maids-of-honor."

"Monica, one of us should be your maid-of-honor and the other two should be bridesmaids." Pam laughed.

"Forget tradition. This is my wedding. I love you all the same, so all of you all will be my maids-of-honor. At least, if you all want to?"

"We wouldn't have it any other way," Kim responded.

***

Monica and Keith exchanged vows before fifty guests exactly two weeks after their proposal.

"You are glowing, darling. I'm so proud of you. I know things haven't always worked out the way you wanted them to, but I guess that has turned around. You did just marry the love of your life." Monica's mom smiled as she smoothed down Monica's hair into the bun. Monica had just changed from her wedding gown in preparation to leave for her honeymoon.

"Thanks, Ma. I love you so much."

"Goodbye, baby."

Kim knocked on the bathroom door letting Monica know that Keith was ready to head to the airport.

The wedding guests wished Keith and Monica well as the couple fled from the reception on the way to their honeymoon. Keith and Monica arrived hours later to their suite in Montego Bay, Jamaica. They didn't waste anytime claiming each other's bodies as their own. Over and over. They never left the suite the entire week they were there.

***

4 months later

"Earth to Monica. I know that you're a newlywed and all, but don't forget that you have friends and new sister-in-laws that love spending time with you, too. Not to mention that you married my brother, so I never see him anymore. You two can come up for air for a while." Kim laughed as she read Monica the riot act. Pam and Renee were on the line as well.

"Whatever, ladies. We've been *busy*." Monica chuckled.

"So, when will we see you again?" Pam asked.

"Soon. We haven't been to the Mellow Lounge in a long time. You all wanna meet up there this Friday night?"

"Will it just be us ladies or will Keith be joining us?" Renee asked.

"Maybe he will, maybe he won't." Monica's laugh suggested that he would.

***

"Monica, are you going to perform tonight? Remember, you never performed the last time we were here," Pam said.

"I remember when all of my poems used to be sad. Now I have a different way to express myself." Monica turned and kissed Keith.

"You so nasty," Kim said and they all laughed.

"Maybe I will, maybe I won't," Monica said jokingly, although she knew she would. It was going to be her first time ever performing in front of them.

"Coming to the stage we have a virgin performer…let's give a round of applause to Monicaaaaaa!"

She laughed as the girls' gasped as she went on stage.

"Whew! How y'all doing out there tonight?" Monica said, trying to engage the audience and calm her nerves all at the same time. "I recently wrote this piece. Here it goes.

I never knew a love like this before
I'm so content with being in your arms
God showed me what true love was right before we
*   got together*
Waking up to you every morning is like heaven on
*   earth*
A new heaven where God supplies all of our needs
*   with promises to give us the desires of hearts*

The very thing that threatened to keep me from
marrying you is only going to bring us closer
He knew what my desire was for you, for us
Keith, I'm carrying your seed

Monica smiled and waved at the other patrons applauding her as she rubbed her growing belly. She exited the stage and returned to her table. Pam, Kim, Renee, and Keith sat in shock each of them varying with their eyes bulging, holding their breath, or just staring at Monica as she took her seat.

Kim came out of her almost catatonic state and spoke up first for the group, "Monica your poem was beautiful, but what was it about? Honey, are you alright?" she asked nervously.

"I'm more than alright. Didn't you all hear me? I'm pregnant."

They were all too nervous to be excited just yet.

Keith grabbed Monica's hands and stared into her eyes. "Baby, didn't you tell me that you couldn't get pregnant? That we'd have to adopt? So, how are you pregnant?"

Monica smiled with pure happiness. "Baby, apparently those University doctors didn't know what they were talking about. I've been so happy with being your wife that it just dawned on me that I haven't had a period since the week before we got married. I got nervous, thinking that it was further complications from my abortion. I didn't want to alarm you, so I didn't say anything to you until I had the doctor to check me out. I went in today and explained my medical history and that I missed my period for the last four months unknowingly. The first thing the doctor recommended was for me to take a pregnancy test. I informed him that there was no need for that. He said he would do one anyway and proceeded to check my uterus and cervix for the complications that my medical file listed from the University. About an hour into the exam a nurse returned to the room. She gave the doctor my pregnancy test results. I told him that he didn't have to bother telling me that I wasn't pregnant, I already knew I wasn't." Monica began to cry. "He said, 'Mrs. Williams, I don't know why those doctors at the University told you what they did, but I have been inspecting your uterus and cervix and I couldn't find any of the complications they listed you as having, not to mention that the pregnancy test came back positive.' I was shocked when my doctor told me that I was pregnant. I begged him to stop playing with me. He said that since I estimated my last period to be three months ago then I should be along far enough to have an ultra sound. He had a nurse to prep me for it and before I knew it I was listening to the heartbeat of two babies." Monica stared at Keith and smiled.

ANITA DAVIS

Keith sat with his eyebrows furrowed and his mouth gaped wide open the entire time Monica shared her story. He finally said, "Wait, what? Two heartbeats?"

It took Keith a minute to grasp what Monica had shared with him. She was having his babies. Two of them at the same time. He didn't care where he was at that moment. He kissed her passionately while Pam and his sisters congratulated them and shed tears of joy.

Other Books Available

Sisterhood Chronicles Series
Underneath It All
Discovery
Untold
When It Happens To You
All Things Considered

Forever Friends Series
Catch Me If You Can
It's Complicated

Limelight Series
Hues
Tones

Standalone Titles
After All Is Said & Done
The Bid Catcher: Distinguished Gentlemen Series

(Best if you read Forever Friends series before reading Sisterhood Chronicles 3)

COMING SOON

The Kissing Game: Love Alive 1

ABOUT THE AUTHOR

Anita Davis is a former elementary teacher born and raised in Chicago. Although she wrote short stories much of her childhood, she didn't unlock and cultivate her passion as a writer until she became a writing teacher for middle school students. The more she had to create sample writings for her students, the more she realized her passion and ability to tell stories in the written form. She decided to hone her craft as a writer by completing her Master of Fine Arts in Creative Writing via National University. She now pursues writing books most of her time, in addition to being a flight attendant. Anita seeks to encourage, engage, and entertain her readers.

She is Co-Founder of Book Euphoria, a group of Chicago authors bound by their love of literature. Book Euphoria hosts literary events and they also founded the empowerment movement, Black Girl Passion.

Anita writes women's fiction fused with clean, contemporary romantic women's fiction and seeks to encourage, engage, and entertain her readers.

authoranitadavis@gmail.com
www.authoranitadavis.com
Facebook: Anita Davis and Author page: Author Anita Davis
Instagram: @authoranitadavis   Twitter: @_AnitaDavis